I0933874

Published by
Princeton Architectural Press
A division of Chronicle Books LLC
70 West 36th Street
New York, NY 10018 www.papress.com

Text & illustrations © 2022 Marianne Dubuc
(original title: *Chacun son tour!*)
Published with the permission of Éditions Album Inc.
6520 Christophe-Colomb
Montréal, Quebec H2S 2G8, Canada
All rights reserved

Translation rights arranged through the VeroK
Agency, Barcelona, Spain

English edition © 2024 Princeton Architectural Press
Printed and bound in China
27 26 25 24 4 3 2 1 First edition

ISBN 978-1-7972-2729-0

Every reasonable attempt has been made to identify
owners of copyright. Errors or omissions will be
corrected in subsequent editions.

This book was illustrated using ink, watercolor, and
colored pencil.

For Princeton Architectural Press:
Editor: Holly La Due
Typesetting: Natalie Snodgrass
Translator: Celyn Harding-Jones

Library of Congress Cataloging-in-Publication Data
available upon request.

marianne dubuc

Everyone Gets a Turn

Hello!

PA PRESS

PRINCETON ARCHITECTURAL PRESS · NEW YORK

In the heart of the forest, on a beautiful day, four little friends play. Turtle reads her favorite book and Hare eats her snack.

Go a little farther, I'll throw you the ball.

Here?

But Bear doesn't know his own strength.

It's too high for Mouse!

After the ball game ends, the friends all go home.

Bye!

Just as Mouse lights the fireplace, he hears a little voice.

I'M COLD!

Mouse gives his scarf to the egg.

Mouse lends his hat.

Now that Mouse has taken good care of the egg, the two warm up and chat by the fire.

It's getting late.

It's time to sleep, Little Egg.

Your blanket looks cozy.

Yes, it is. I like it a lot.

I'll share it with you.

Little Egg is happy and sleeps soundly in the warmth of Mouse's house.

Morning comes and Mouse hurries to bring Little Egg to Bear's house.

You have your blanket, it will keep you warm.

It was hard for Bear to be patient waiting for Little Egg.

It's your turn!

Bear always says, "An active body for an active brain."

1...2...1...2...

Hop! Hop! Hop!

Humph!

All of a sudden...

CRACK!

But Little Egg is not strong enough.

The other day I used a stick to lift up a big rock that was too heavy. Do you have a stick in there?

Little Egg starts to think.

Little Egg pushes with her brain and with her little muscles.

After all her efforts, Little Egg has become an exhausted Little Bird.

HARE'S
HOUSE

Bear brings the sleeping Little Bird to Hare's house.

But where is Little Egg?

Shh.

Bear explains to Hare how Little Egg became Little Bird.

She is so small.

She worked very hard and she got here all by herself!

Just as Hare finishes reading the morning news, Little Bird wakes up.

I'M HUNGRY!

Hare wonders what a Little Bird eats.

It seems a carrot is not going to cut it.

Hare offers a clover leaf to Little Bird.

Hare shows Little Bird her pantry.
Maybe we don't like the same things.
WHOA!

So Little Bird tries all sorts of things.

And she discovers what she likes.

OM NOM!
OM NOM!

TURTLE'S
HOUSE

With a full belly, Little Bird runs along the road to Turtle's house.

Not too fast!

Turtle happily welcomes Little Bird.

I'm big and I'm no longer hungry.

Can I see your house?

There are all sorts of mysterious objects at Turtle's house.

Turtle lets Little Bird explore.

It sparkles!

It's tiny!

Are these magic?

Maybe.

WOW!

Little Bird is filled with wonder.

Turtle and Little Bird drink tea and tell each other incredible stories.

TURTLE'S HOUSE
(again)

After a good night's sleep, Turtle is excited to tell her dreams to Little Bird.

It was amazing!

But Little Bird's bed is empty.

Little Bird! You'll never guess the dream I ha-....

WHERE ARE YOU?

Mouse arrives first.

Where is she?

Bear and Hare are worried.

Did you find her?

She is lost!

Poor Little Bird!

BOOHOO!

All of a sudden...

I'm here!

But you will be alone without us.

I'll visit you every day.

But you are so small...

Now I know how to take care of myself.

Look at the pulley I made!

LITTLE BIRD'S HOUSE

This is my house!

Little Bird is all set up in her house, and now it's her turn to invite her friends over.

I'll try the pulley.

I have a good story to tell you.

I brought you a cake.

And I knitted you some mittens.

Oh, thank you!

Hmmmm...

Little Bird doesn't like that name.

She thinks for a moment.

I think I'd like to be called CLARA!

The friends are surprised, but then...

Good idea!

A little bit later, after they leave Clara's house, the friends wonder what their names would be if they weren't Bear, Hare, Turtle, and Mouse.

And that's how Clara and her friends all learned from each other.
Tomorrow they will continue to grow, each in their own way.